Dear Parent:

Congratulations! Your child is taking the first steps on an exciting journey. The destination? Independent reading!

STEP INTO READING® will help your child get there. The program offers five steps to reading success. Each step includes fun stories and colorful art. There are also Step into Reading Sticker Books, Step into Reading Math Readers, Step into Reading Phonics Readers, Step into Reading Write-In Readers, and Step into Reading Phonics Boxed Sets—a complete literacy program with something for every child.

Learning to Read, Step by Step!

Ready to Read   Preschool–Kindergarten
• big type and easy words • rhyme and rhythm • picture clues
For children who know the alphabet and are eager to begin reading.

Reading with Help   Preschool–Grade 1
• basic vocabulary • short sentences • simple stories
For children who recognize familiar words and sound out new words with help.

Reading on Your Own   Grades 1–3
• engaging characters • easy-to-follow plots • popular topics
For children who are ready to read on their own.

Reading Paragraphs   Grades 2–3
• challenging vocabulary • short paragraphs • exciting stories
For newly independent readers who read simple sentences with confidence.

Ready for Chapters   Grades 2–4
• chapters • longer paragraphs • full-color art
For children who want to take the plunge into chapter books but still like colorful pictures.

STEP INTO READING® is designed to give every child a successful reading experience. The grade levels are only guides. Children can progress through the steps at their own speed, developing confidence in their reading, no matter what their grade.

Remember, a lifetime love of reading starts with a single step!

Stephen Hillenburg

Based on the TV series *SpongeBob SquarePants*® created by Stephen Hillenburg as seen on Nickelodeon®

Visit us on the Web!
StepIntoReading.com
randomhouse.com/kids

Educators and librarians, for a variety of teaching tools, visit us at RHTeachersLibrarians.com

ISBN: 978-0-449-81438-3 (trade) — ISBN: 978-0-375-97159-4 (lib. bdg.)
Printed in the United States of America
10 9 8 7 6 5 4

STEP INTO READING®

STEP 2

DANCING WITH THE STAR

By Alex Harvey
Illustrated by Stephen Reed

Random House 🏠 New York

Pearl watches TV.

Her favorite show

is a dance contest.

Mr. Krabs sees the host.

The host is his friend!

Pearl wants to have

a dance contest

with the host!

"What a great idea!"
says Mr. Krabs.

Mr. Krabs invites
his friend.

He can host the contest.

It will be at the
Krusty Krab.

SpongeBob and
Squidward
are very excited.

Squidward wants to win the contest!

SpongeBob and
Squidward
hang flyers
all over town.

Sandy wants to win
with the Texas two-step.

Larry the Lobster
practices
the cha-cha.

Patrick wants to enter
the contest.
But he is scared.

DANCE
CONTEST
AT THE
KRUSTY KRAB

SpongeBob decides
to help his friend.

Patrick and SpongeBob
go to SpongeBob's house.

SpongeBob puts on music.

Patrick twists.

He flops.

He falls on his face!

Patrick needs help.

SpongeBob will train
Patrick!

SpongeBob helps Patrick.

Patrick runs.

He sweats.

He learns ballet.

He dances!

The contest begins.

Everyone is

at the Krusty Krab.

The cameras roll.

The host

greets the crowd.

The judges are ready!

Squidward goes first.

He twirls.

He gets tangled up!

Sandy is next.

She dances.

She is great!

Larry does the cha-cha.

He is very good.

It is Patrick's turn.

He is nervous.

SpongeBob gives Patrick
the thumbs-up!

Patrick starts.

He boogies.

He flips

across the floor.

Patrick is the best!

He wins the contest!

Patrick is a dance star!